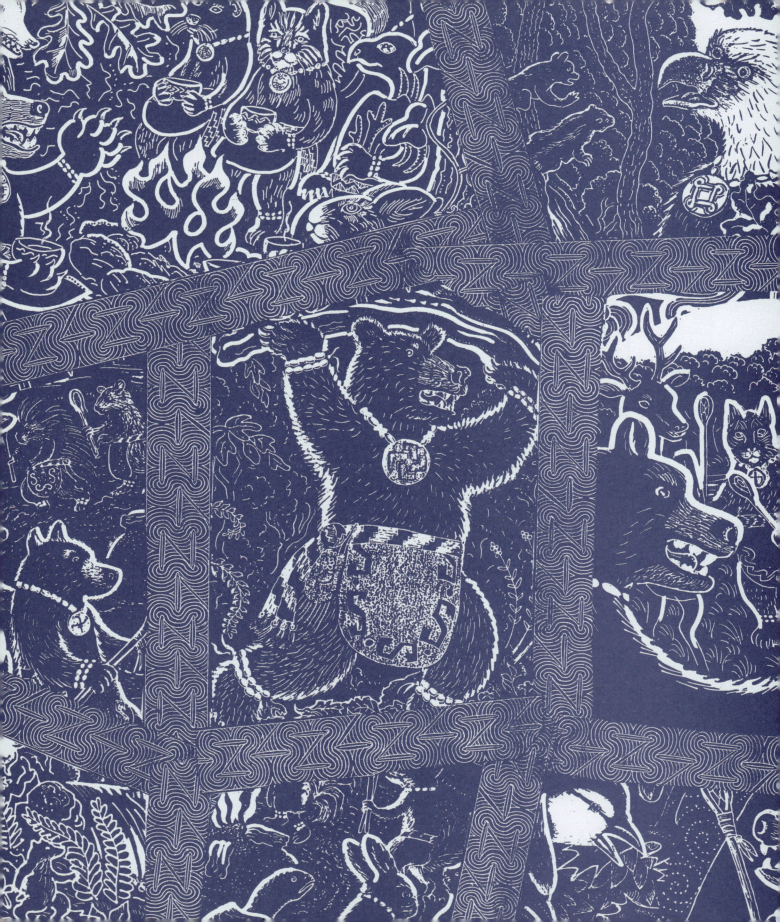

The Great Ball Game
of the Birds and Animals

The Great Ball Game of the Birds and Animals

Volume 1 of the Grandmother Stories

drawings by
Murv Jacob

story by
Deborah L. Duvall

University of New Mexico Press
Albuquerque

Dedication

To Robin Aurora Star, the Christmas baby.

Library of Congress Cataloging-in-Publication Data

Duvall, Deborah L., 1952–
The great ball game of the birds and animals / story by Deborah L. Duvall ;
drawings by Murv Jacob.—1st ed.
p.   cm.   —   (Grandmother stories ; v. 1)
Summary: When Bear and Terrapin tell two small furry animals that they cannot compete in the important stickball game between the animals and the birds, the two are welcomed by the birds, who find a way for them to fly.
ISBN 0-8263-2913-6 (cloth : alk. paper)
1. Cherokee Indians—Folklore.   2. Tales—Southern States.
[1. Cherokee Indians—Folklore.   2. Indians of North America—Folklore.]
I. Jacob, Murv, ill.   II. Title.   III. Series.
E99.C5 D89 2002
398.2'089'9755—dc21

Printed in Tokyo

In those days . . .

. . . the Animals decided to challenge
the Birds to a game of stickball.

"Hurry!" the little creature shouted to his tiny companion. "We must keep up with them!"

For hours they had followed the group of large animals who walked the wide path above them. These creatures, too, were in a hurry, because the ceremonial grounds lay just ahead.

The furry little animals, no bigger than mice, listened intently to all the talk about the big game to take place the next morning. The Animals had challenged the Birds to a game of stickball, and the winners of this match would be very great indeed!

Of course, the Animals believed they would win. They were much bigger and stronger than the Birds. Suddenly, Bear, the captain of the Animals, let out a tremendous roar. He picked up a huge log and held it above his head.

"This is what I will do to any Bird who tries to take the ball from me!" he yelled.

Then he heaved the log away and sent it crashing down the mountainside. The tiny animals watched with terror and amazement as the log whizzed over their heads. Then, before the noise died away, they heard a loud chuckle from above. It was the great Terrapin, standing up on his hind legs, hooting and cheering on his teammate.

"And I," laughed Terrapin, "will do this to any bird who gets in my way!"

With that, he lunged forward, landing flat on the ground. The heavy jolt shook the earth beneath him. Then he jumped up and threw himself down again, bringing a great round of approving shouts from his friends.

Deer had been prancing along, in and out of the crowd, and suddenly he began to sing.

"I'm quicker than the eye can see. No one is as fast as me!"

Then he was off, swift as an arrow! As he disappeared down the path, everyone began to race toward the dance grounds and the great river beyond. The two tiny creatures ran behind them, as fast as their little legs could go.

When they finally reached the river, Bear was standing atop a big

rock near the dance grounds. He was choosing the players for his stickball team. This was the moment the little animals had been waiting for! But now they were afraid. Now they had to ask the great Bear's permission to be members of the team.

Bear bent down with a puzzled look to the brown little things, who called to him.

"What is it you want?" he asked, as quietly as he could. "I am busy selecting my team."

"Oh, great Bear, we are small. But we are quick and brave. We want to be part of your team." The tiny ones trembled as they made the request. "We want to play stickball with the Animals."

"Ho!" Bear roared so loudly the little animals rolled backward several times. "So you want to play ball with us! Go and find a safe place to hide and watch us win this game!"

His loud laughter followed them all the way back to the path. As they neared the forest, the two unhappy creatures heard chattering and chirping coming from the treetops. Then all at once came the rushing sound of wings, as the Birds formed a graceful circle in the air. The Birds were dancing to prepare for the game!

"The Animals do not want us," said the smaller of the two, "so we will play stickball for the Birds. We must climb up and speak with Eagle. He is their captain. Perhaps he will allow us to join his team."

They watched carefully as the Birds finished dancing to spot the exact tree on which Eagle perched. Then they began to climb. Up they went, each clutching to the tree bark. At last they reached the very top of the tree where Eagle sat upon a strong branch.

"Oh mighty Eagle," they called to the powerful bird. "We wish to join you in the game against the Animals. We are small, but we are quick and brave. We will help you to defeat them."

Eagle was surprised when the two scurried up to his branch. Why, they were no bigger than Sparrow!

"But you have four feet," he said to them. "And where are your wings? You must be Animals. So why do you not play for their team?"

"We spoke to the great Bear," one replied. "And he only laughed at us and drove us away."

Eagle thought for a long time.

"Yes, I would like to have you for my team," he decided. "But how can you help us if you cannot fly?"

Just then Bluejay flew over from a nearby limb. Now Bluejay was the nosiest of all the Birds. He listened and watched and always knew everything that was going on in the world. It only took a moment for him to answer.

"Let's make them some wings!"

"Good," Eagle said. "But we had better hurry."

Night had fallen and a full moon lit the treetops. From a distance, they could hear the Animals howling and roaring. Their ball dance had begun.

The craftiest of all the Birds were called on to help make the wings. Bluejay cut two small pieces of groundhog skin from the head of their dance drum. Martin and Raven flew down to the water and returned with a section of river cane. This they stripped into splints.

The splints were fastened to the forelegs of the smallest furry creature. Then the groundhog skin was stretched across the splints and attached to his front feet. Now he had a beautiful set of wings!

Then Eagle gave him a name. From that day, he was to be called "Tla-me-ha," the Bat. He and Bluejay took turns darting through the trees with a game ball.

Eagle was pleased with his newest team member. But now they must design another set of wings for his friend. All the skin from the dance drum had been used. Again, it was Bluejay who came up with the answer.

"Look here at this skin on his sides," said Bluejay. "If we pull and stretch the skin toward his feet, I think this little one can fly."

The tiny creature held tightly to the tree limb as three birds gathered on each side of his body. Gently, they began to tug and pull at the skin on his sides until it stretched away from his body and legs. Now he could sail through the air by holding all four feet outstretched.

Eagle said, "You, too, shall have a new name. From now on, you will be called 'Te-wa,' the Flying Squirrel."

The next morning, Hawk, who had been keeping watch from the tallest tree, gave his signal cry. The stickball game was about to begin. At once all the Birds echoed with loud shrieks. The Animals were waiting at the riverbank. They all screamed back a reply. This yelling back and forth went on until both teams reached the playing field.

"Look over there," said Bluejay to Bat and Flying Squirrel. "You see the two poles in the ground behind the Animals? To win, we must carry the ball between those poles."

In front of the poles stood Terrapin and Bear, looking bigger than ever before! Bluejay pointed to another set of poles at the far side of the field.

"Those are the poles that we must defend. The animals will try to reach them."

The Birds took their places in the trees just above their goal poles. Everyone was tense and ready to begin. Rabbit, the Trickster, had been chosen to start the game. He stood in the center of the field. Terrapin, Deer, and Bear waited near him at the very edge of their boundary.

For a moment, all was silent. Every eye was turned to the ball in Rabbit's paw. He looked from the Birds to the Animals, and then back again. He also looked for a quick escape route from the paths of Terrapin and Bear. Suddenly, he threw the ball high, high into the air, then dashed for the safety of the trees.

The ball was coming down again, fast! Terrapin and Bear jumped for it at the same instant. But Terrapin wanted that ball! He slapped Bear down with his powerful arm, then jumped on Bear's back. The ball was headed straight into his woven stick. But then it was gone!

Something furry and brown had snatched the ball right out of his reach and carried it to a nearby tree. It was Flying Squirrel! Terrapin did not have much time to think about this, because Bear jumped up with a mighty heave and flung the big turtle on his back, leaving him helpless in the middle of the field.

From the tree, Flying Squirrel whistled to Bat, who caught the spinning ball just above the heads of Wolf and Deer. Deer leaped as high as he could, thrusting his horns into the air. But Bat darted in and out of the deadly horns and soon had Deer turning circles in the field. Then he tossed the ball to Bluejay.

Bluejay headed straight toward the goal poles with the heavy ball in his beak and Bear's slashing claws just beneath him. He was getting closer and closer to victory when a loud racket made him look sideways into the forest. It was Rabbit, banging on his drum and yelling at the top of his lungs! Then Bluejay, who knew everything, dropped the ball!

Rabbit was hopping up and down with pride as Bear hurried after the fallen ball. But Martin was faster! Bear's stick just missed her as she fluttered over his head and pitched the ball to Bat.

This time Bat did not take any chances. Holding tightly to the ball, he flapped his little leather wings and rose high into the air. Then he began to dive, gaining speed as he went, and carried the ball through the poles, passing right in front of the mighty Bear.

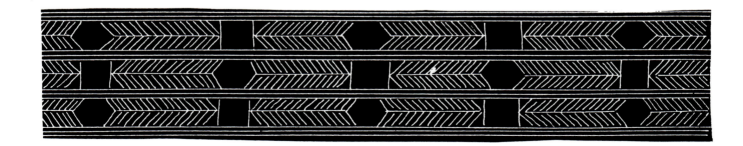

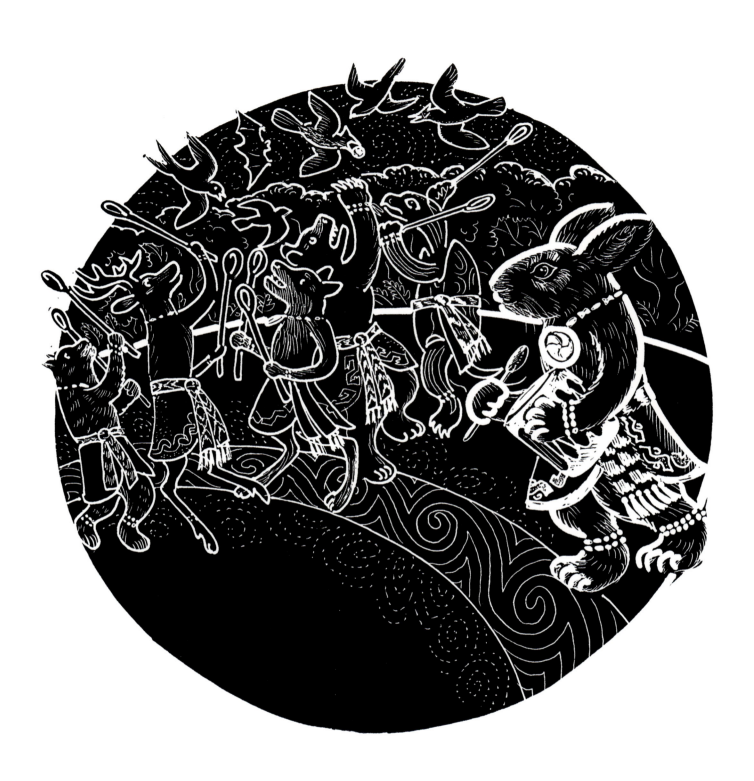

The Birds had won the stickball game!

For several days, the Birds feasted and celebrated their great victory. For her bravery in saving the ball from Bear, the Birds gave Martin a beautiful painted gourd in which to make her home. And even now, she still has it.

Flying Squirrel made his home in the trees, very close to the cave where his good friend Bat would now live. And Bluejay, who knew everything, said that the stickball game between the Birds and the Animals was the finest game ever played. And, as usual, he was right!

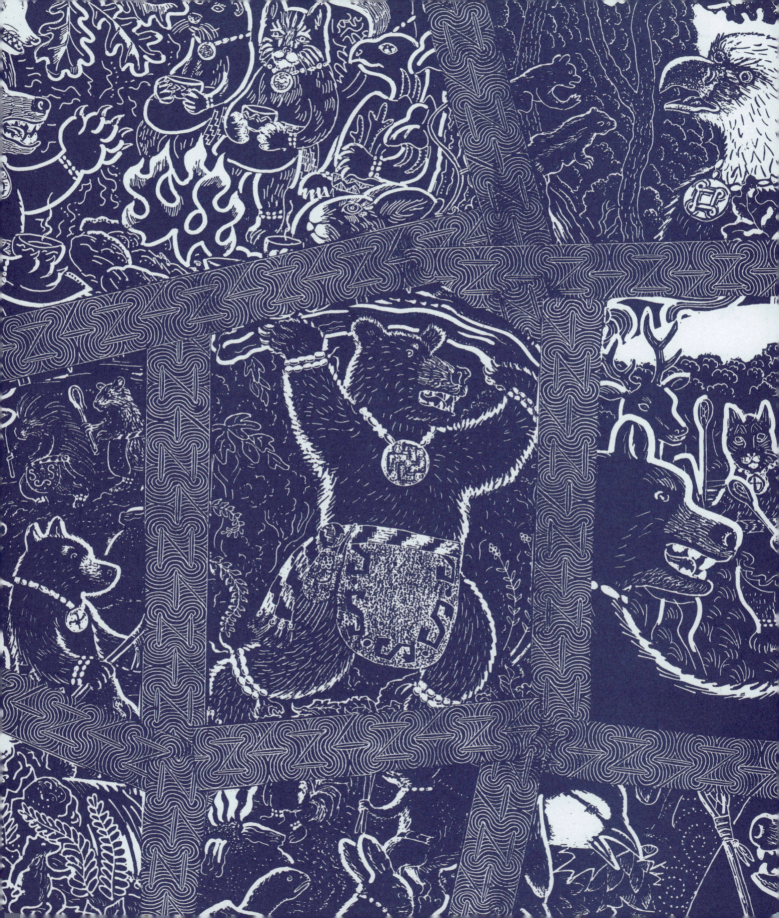